This Book Belongs to:

Easter Bunny
Are You For Real?

Harold Myra

ILLUSTRATED BY JANE KURISU

Tommy
NELSON

Thomas Nelson, Inc.

Nashville

This is a revised edition of the book by the same title previously
published in 1979 by Thomas Nelson, Inc., Publishers.

Text copyright © 1979, 1998 by Harold Myra
Illustrations copyright © 1998 by Tommy Nelson™,
a division of Thomas Nelson, Inc.

Published in Nashville, Tennessee, by Tommy Nelson™, a division of Thomas Nelson, Inc.

Library of Congress Cataloging-in-Publication Data

Myra, Harold Lawrence, 1939–
     Easter bunny are you for real? / Harold Myra : illustrated by Jane Kurisu.
          p.   cm.
     Summary: Three children learn about the origins of the Easter bunny
and other symbols and customs associated with Easter.
     ISBN 0-8499-1493-0
     [1. Easter—Fiction.] I. Kurisu, Jane, 1952–   ill. II. Title.
PZ7.M9954Eas   1998
[E]—dc21

                                                                    97–32656
                                                                         CIP
                                                                          AC

Printed in the United States of America

00 01 02 03   BVG   9 8 7 6 5 4 3

A Note to Parents

Easter eggs, Easter bunnies, Easter parades. Children see animated characters, hear silly stories, and shout with glee in egg hunts during the spring "holiday" season.

How can girls and boys see beyond commercialism and cuddly, cutesy stuff and grasp what the early church considered the celebration? Christ is risen! He is risen indeed!

It is my hope that this book will help children sort out the festivities and find the Easter that is at the heart of our Christian faith.

—Harold Myra

"Look at that funny bunny," Mom said.

"No!" Greg declared. "Bad bunny."

"Now where did you hear that?" Dad asked.

"Bad bunny," Greg repeated very seriously, shaking his head from side to side. "Bad."

Greg was too young to tell his mom and dad what he meant. Dad asked Michelle and Todd, "Where did Greg get the idea that the Easter Bunny is bad?"

Michelle and Todd thought awhile. Finally Michelle said, "I remember someone at church saying it's a shame the way kids get all excited about the Easter Bunny."

"Why shouldn't we get excited about the Easter Bunny?" Todd asked.

"What does the Easter Bunny have to do with Easter? We never talk about the Easter Bunny in Sunday school," Michelle added.

"Well," said Dad, "let's go back to the beginning. Jesus' friends saw him killed on the cross, then buried. What a terrible day! Jesus was dead.

"But three days later—
that first Easter dawn—
Jesus rose from his grave.
He was alive again!

"His disciples suddenly understood what Jesus had been trying to tell them. Death is the beginning, not the end. Jesus would live forever. And they would, too!"

"But what about the Easter Bunny?" Michelle interrupted.

"The Easter Bunny has nothing to do with the real Easter," said Dad. "The Easter Bunny—along with new leaves and flowers and new baby kittens and baby chicks—is part of how we celebrate spring. But that's all. Spring is God's picture of Jesus rising from the dead as all of nature comes to life again."

"Where did the eggs come in?" Mom called from the kitchen as she spooned hard-cooked eggs out of a pot. Michelle and Todd and Greg scrambled to the kitchen table to pick their favorite colors.

"The season before Easter, Christians remembered the sufferings of Jesus. Many gave up certain foods, including eggs. We call this time *Lent*.

"When Easter arrived each year, Christians celebrated their new life in Christ. The sad time of not eating was over. It was time for the Easter feast.

"Years ago, because eggs made people think of new life, they were brought to the table colored red for Easter joy."

"I'm getting mixed up," Michelle objected.
"I don't remember eggs in the Bible stories."

"You're right, Michelle," said Dad.
"The real Easter and all the springtime
fun got mixed together.

"For hundreds of years people have been hiding eggs and telling stories of how the Easter Bunny burns wild flowers to make dye. There are a lot of other stories about Easter, too. Some people used to say that the sun skipped for joy every Easter morning and that if you got up early you'd see it."

"Hiding eggs is fun," said Greg.

"Is it okay to celebrate spring like that?" asked Todd.

"Sure — if we also remember that on the real Easter Jesus rose from the dead!"

The next morning *very early*, while it was still dark, the three children and their parents went sleepily to the patio to wait for the Easter sunrise and remember Jesus.

Slowly, slowly, a bit of pink light began on the horizon.

"I *love* the Easterrise," Greg said.

Mom and Dad smiled.

"You know," Dad said, "in the early days of the church, Jesus' rising from the dead was so important that every Sunday was celebrated as Easter."

"Then let's get to church and celebrate," said Mom.

After church, Michelle, Todd, and Greg sampled a piece of their Easter candy. Greg pointed to a chocolate bunny in a candy box. "Bad bunny," he said again.

"Greg's right," Michelle declared. "People think about the Easter Bunny and forget the real Easter."

"Yeah, that's crazy!" said Todd.

"Think about the Easter Bunny this way," Dad said. "A rabbit spends the winter in a dark hole in the earth. But in the springtime, the rabbit leaps out of that hole, full of life. That is how we have been set free by our risen Lord Jesus."

Greg was munching the ears off his chocolate bunny.

"Well," Todd said, "the Easter Bunny got us talking a lot about God and Jesus this year."

"Yes," Dad agreed. "And since God made both bunnies and food, I think I'll have a little bite, too."

And he did.